PRESENTS

THE AMERICAN GIRLS COLLECTION

18 54

MEET KIRSTEN · An American Girl
KIRSTEN LEARNS A LESSON · A School Story
KIRSTEN'S SURPRISE · A Christmas Story
HAPPY BIRTHDAY, KIRSTEN! · A Springtime Story
KIRSTEN SAVES THE DAY · A Summer Story
CHANGES FOR KIRSTEN · A Winter Story

19 04

MEET SAMANTHA · An American Girl
SAMANTHA LEARNS A LESSON · A School Story
SAMANTHA'S SURPRISE · A Christmas Story
HAPPY BIRTHDAY, SAMANTHA! · A Springtime Story
SAMANTHA SAVES THE DAY · A Summer Story
CHANGES FOR SAMANTHA · A Winter Story

19 44

MEET MOLLY · An American Girl
MOLLY LEARNS A LESSON · A School Story
MOLLY'S SURPRISE · A Christmas Story
HAPPY BIRTHDAY, MOLLY! · A Springtime Story
MOLLY SAVES THE DAY · A Summer Story
CHANGES FOR MOLLY · A Winter Story

SAMANTHA
LEARNS
A LESSON
A SCHOOL STORY

BY SUSAN S. ADLER

ILLUSTRATIONS NANCY NILES, R. GRACE

VIGNETTES EILEEN POTTS DAWSON

SCHOLASTIC INC.

NEW YORK   TORONTO   LONDON   AUCKLAND   SYDNEY

PICTURE CREDITS
The following individuals and organizations have generously given
permission to reprint illustrations contained in "Looking Back:"
pp. 56–57—State Historical Society of Wisconsin; Courtesy Library of
Congress; pp. 58–59—State Historical Society of Wisconsin; State
Historical Society of Wisconsin; International Museum of Photography at
George Eastman House; The Bettmann Archive; pp. 60–61—Courtesy
Library of Congress; Acme Newspictures; University of Wisconsin-
Madison Archives.

Edited by Jeanne Thieme
Designed by Myland McRevey

ISBN 0-590-43783-6

12 11 10 9 8 7 6 5 4 3 2 1   0 1 2 3 4 5/9

Printed in the U.S.A.
First Scholastic printing, February 1990

TO DAVID, RACHEL,
AND DANIEL, WHO KEEP
CHILDHOOD OPEN TO ME

TABLE OF CONTENTS

Samantha's Family

Grandmary
Samantha's grandmother, who wants her to be a young lady.

Nellie
Samantha's friend who does housework and schoolwork.

Samantha
A nine-year-old orphan who lives with her wealthy grandmother.

Uncle Gard
Samantha's favorite uncle, who calls her Sam.

Cornelia
An old-fashioned beauty who has new-fangled ideas.

HAWKINS
*Grandmary's butler
and driver, who
is Samantha's friend.*

MRS. HAWKINS
*The cook, who
always has a treat
for Samantha.*

JESSIE
*Grandmary's
seamstress, who
"patches
Samantha up."*

ELSA
*The maid, who
is usually grumpy.*

EDDIE
*Samantha's
neighbor who loves
to tease.*

CHAPTER
ONE
—

NOTES AND
KNEE BENDS

Something poked Samantha in the back. Samantha jumped slightly, but she didn't look up. She knew the signal. It was from Helen.

Helen Whitney had the desk behind Samantha's. Both desks were like all the other desks in the classroom at Miss Crampton's Academy for Girls. Their iron sides were molded in lacy swirls and curls. And one particular curl was just the right size for holding notes.

Talking in class was not allowed at Miss Crampton's, so when Helen had something to tell Samantha she would write it on a small piece of paper. Then she would roll the paper up, stick it in

1

the proper iron curl, and poke Samantha in the back with her pencil. Samantha would wait until Miss Stevens wasn't looking, then drop her hand back and pull out the note. Once she caught her finger in the iron swirls and barely got it loose before Miss Stevens turned around. But usually the system worked wonderfully.

Now Samantha waited until the teacher's back was turned. She reached for the note. It said:

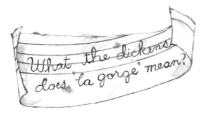

What the dickens does "la gorge" mean?

Samantha looked up quickly, squashed the note small, and shoved it into her pocket. It would be bad enough to be caught passing notes in school. She couldn't imagine what would happen if she were caught with a note that said *the dickens*. Didn't Helen have enough sense not to write almost-swear-words in school?

There wasn't enough time for Samantha to answer Helen's note. Miss Stevens had already finished writing a long list of French words on the

La gorge

blackboard. Now she turned around and faced the class. And she looked straight at Helen.

"Helen, will you please tell us what *la gorge* means?" Miss Stevens asked.

Samantha tried to give Helen a clue. "A-a-ahemm," she cleared her throat rather loudly. Miss Stevens stared at her, then looked back at Helen.

Helen didn't answer, so Samantha tried again. She rubbed the back of her neck.

"Samantha, are you well?" asked Miss Stevens. She was looking at Samantha through gold-rimmed spectacles that seemed to see everything. She looked as if she had a pretty good idea of what was going on.

"Yes, ma'am," said Samantha softly. She folded her hands on her desk. Helen would have to answer on her own.

"Is it the neck?" squeaked Helen uncertainly.

"No, Helen, it is not," said Miss Stevens. She looked around the room. Edith Eddleton stretched her hand high in the air, and Miss Stevens called on her.

"*La gorge*," said Edith smugly, "means the throat."

"That is correct," said Miss Stevens, and Edith gloated. Samantha could just imagine Edith keeping score in her head: "Me—107; Everyone else—0." Edith was smart, but not as smart as she thought she was. Probably no one on earth was as smart as Edith Eddleton thought she was.

The class was just finishing the list of words on the blackboard when the lunch bell rang. The girls stood beside their desks. They waited until Miss Stevens nodded for them to go and get their lunchboxes from the cloakroom. Then they filed quietly out the door.

The day was warm, so the girls could eat outside on the benches in the yard. Helen, Ida Dean, and Ruth Adams waited for Samantha at their usual spot. Samantha squirmed as she sat down next to them. Her legs itched from the long flannel underwear that was tucked under her stockings. But she had to wear it, whether the days were warm or cold. Grandmary said flannel

The day was warm, so the girls could eat outside
on the benches in the yard.

underwear kept children from getting consumption, and she insisted that Samantha put it on at the beginning of September.

"Do you think Miss Crampton will make us do arm stretches today?" Ida asked between bites of her chopped olive sandwich. Miss Crampton was Head of the Academy, and she was very serious about exercise. At one o'clock every day she came to the classroom to lead the girls in exercises. "If she makes us do fifty arm stretches, I'm going to faint," Ida added with a sigh.

"At least arm stretches are better than knee bends," answered Helen. "I hate knee bends. I think Miss Crampton is trying for the world record in knee bends."

"It could be worse," said Ruth. "At my cousin's school they have to practice swimming. But they don't have any water. They have to hang with big ropes around their waists. Then they have to kick and paddle. Just hanging in the air like that."

Ida looked at her in disbelief. "Oh, they never!" she gasped.

Ruth nodded importantly. "I swear it. They do." And she licked jelly neatly off her fingers.

The girls were quiet for a moment, all giving silent thanks for the swimming hole in Mount Bedford. At least they could learn to swim in *real* water. "Maybe knee bends aren't so bad after all," Ida finally said.

Samantha took a gingerbread cookie out of her lunchbox and grew quiet while the other girls talked on. Every time she had gingerbread, Samantha thought about Nellie. Samantha had given Nellie her first taste of gingerbread last summer, when Nellie worked next door at the Rylands' house. But Mrs. Ryland sent Nellie back to the city. Now Samantha missed her friend. She thought about Nellie every day. She remembered all the things Nellie had told her about her life in the city, and she worried.

Nellie had said her whole family—all five of them—lived in one room in a crowded building. There was only one window in the room, and the air always smelled bad. In the summer the room was very hot, and in the winter it was terribly cold. There was a little stove for cooking, but there was never enough coal to make the room warm. And

Nellie had said they were nearly always hungry, because there wasn't enough money.

Samantha remembered all the things Nellie had told her, and the gingerbread tasted dry in her mouth.

As she swallowed the last of her milk, Samantha's thoughts were jerked back to the schoolyard by the ringing of Miss Crampton's bell. She hurried to get in line with the other girls. They all marched back inside to face another afternoon beginning with Miss Crampton's knee bends.

CHAPTER
TWO
—
NELLIE

On Saturday morning Samantha was
getting dressed when there was a sharp
knock at her door. Elsa leaned her head
in. "You have company, miss," she said. Elsa
looked annoyed at having to bother with
Samantha's company. "Your grandmother said to
tell you it's a friend. She's in the parlor." Samantha
was surprised. She had lots of friends who came to
play, but Grandmary would never tell any of them
to wait in the parlor. The parlor was only for
grown-up visitors. Samantha hurried downstairs.
She stopped in the hall to straighten her dress, then
slowly opened the parlor door and looked around.
At first she thought the room was empty. Then she

saw a wide blue bow just peeking over the back of the green velvet chair. That was enough.

"Nellie!" Samantha yelled. She ran around the chair and hugged the girl who jumped up to meet her. Nellie was laughing.

"Oh, Nellie, it's really you! You're all right!" Samantha stood back and looked at her friend. "Are you back at the Rylands'?" she asked.

"Oh, no, it's much better," Nellie said. Her eyes were sparkling. "It was your grandmother, Samantha. She did it. She talked to Mrs. Van Sicklen, and Mrs. Van Sicklen hired my mother and

10

father. Pa will be her driver. He'll take care of the horses and the garden. Ma will cook and clean and do laundry. And Bridget and Jenny and I will help." Nellie bounced with excitement. She looked as if she had a grand surprise. "And guess what, Samantha? We get to *live* there! All of us! We really do! In the rooms over the carriage house. Isn't that wonderful?"

Samantha grabbed Nellie's hands and danced with her around the parlor. "Oh, Nellie! You'll live only two houses away. We can play every single day when I get home from school."

Nellie stopped. Only her eyes danced now. She leaned over as if to tell a secret. "Samantha," she said in an excited half-whisper, "I'm going to go to school, too. Mrs. Van Sicklen told your grandmother I could." Nellie jumped a little jump and clapped her hands. "What do you think of that?"

Samantha hugged her. "Oh, Nellie, that *is* wonderful. It's just wonderful! I'm so glad you're back!" Samantha swung Nellie around in a circle and then started toward the door. "Come on," she called, "maybe Mrs. Hawkins will give us some gingerbread!"

Monday morning Samantha led a strange parade down the hill, across Main Street, and into the Mount Bedford Public School. She walked tall and proud, dressed in her best gray dress. Nellie walked next to her, skipping little excited skips now and then. Jenny and Bridget, Nellie's little sisters, followed behind. They squeezed each other's hands and walked very quietly.

Bridget was seven and Jenny was six. They would both start in the first grade. They looked shy and scared as they tiptoed into their classroom.

Then Samantha led Nellie to the second grade classroom. Nellie would start there because she knew her letters and she could read a little, even though she had never been to school before. In the dim hallway, facing the tall oak door, Nellie looked frightened. She twisted her hand in her dress and looked at Samantha for help. "Everything will be fine, you'll see," Samantha said. "Remember, I'll meet you on the front steps when school's over."

Nellie took a deep breath and stepped into her

classroom. Samantha hurried out of the building and ran the two blocks to Miss Crampton's.

All day long Samantha worried about Nellie. During morning exercises she wished she had taught Nellie the Oath of Allegiance. She knew they would be saying it in the public school. Did Nellie know it? Did she know the hymns they would sing?

At lunchtime, as Samantha ate her watercress sandwich, she remembered the lard pails Nellie and her sisters had carried as lunchboxes. She wished she had looked inside. She wasn't sure they had enough to eat. At least she could have given them her cookies.

 During penmanship class, Samantha practiced S's and Q's and thought that she should have stayed longer with Nellie. Would someone help her find the pencil sharpener? Would there be someone to show her where the bathroom was?

By three o'clock Samantha was almost bursting to know how Nellie had gotten along. She ran the two blocks to the public school and climbed the front steps two at a time. Jenny and Bridget began jumping up and down the minute they saw her. Both of them talked at once.

"There are thirty desks in our room, Samantha. I can count to thirty," Bridget said.

"I have my own desk," Jenny added.

"We put our lunches in the clock room," Bridget continued.

"No, Bridget, it's not a clock room, it's a *cloak* room," said Samantha.

"We have books, see?" Jenny held up three books strapped together with a leather belt.

"That's nice, Jenny," said Samantha. "But where's Nellie? Why isn't she here?"

The little girls looked at each other and shrugged. "We don't know. We haven't seen her."

Samantha looked around. All the other boys and girls were on their way home. Samantha saw Eddie Ryland pulling Carrie Wilson's hair ribbon off and running down the street with it. But there was no sign of Nellie. Where could she be?

Then Samantha saw her. Nellie was huddled by the bushes near the foot of the steps. She was sitting on her heels with her head in her hands. And she was crying.

The three girls ran down the steps and crouched next to Nellie. Jenny and Bridget began patting their sister's back and stroking her hair. Samantha put her arm around Nellie. "What is it? What's the matter?" she asked.

"I can't do it, Samantha," Nellie sobbed. "I'm too old to start school. I can't do it."

"But Nellie, what happened?"

"The children all laughed at me because I'm big and I'm just in second grade," said Nellie as she lifted her tear-stained face. "The teacher made me sit at the back of the room. And she got mad at me when I couldn't get the right answer. She asked me where the Atlantic Ocean was, and I was just so scared that I forgot. Then the children laughed even more." Nellie shuddered with a little sob. "They called me ragbag. And one time when a boy passed my desk he leaned over and whispered 'dummy.'" Nellie hid her face in her lap again. "Oh, Samantha, I can't go back tomorrow," she sobbed.

"Yes you can, Nellie," Samantha said firmly. She was angry now. She was very angry. And when Samantha was angry she was not likely to sit still.

"Nellie, do you know the way home by yourself?" Samantha asked. Nellie nodded. "Well then, you take Jenny and Bridget home. I have to do something. Dry your eyes. It's going to be all right. I promise you it's going to be all right."

Nellie rubbed her hand over her eyes and sniffed loudly. But she got up, took her sisters' hands, and started home. Samantha marched back to Miss Crampton's Academy.

CHAPTER
THREE
—
MOUNT BETTER
SCHOOL

Miss Stevens was at her desk. She was busy writing something, but she stopped when she saw Samantha. "Can I help you, Samantha?" she asked.

"Yes, Miss Stevens," answered Samantha. She did not know quite how to begin. At last she said, "I have a friend, and she's just started school. She's nine, but she never went to school because she had to work in a factory. She's in the second grade." Samantha stopped and watched Miss Stevens closely to see if she would think this was funny. But Miss Stevens didn't look as if she thought there was anything funny at all.

Samantha went on. "The children tease her and

17

the teacher is mean. She thinks my friend isn't very smart. But she *is* smart, Miss Stevens. She just needs help."

Miss Stevens nodded, so Samantha kept talking. "I could teach her, but I don't know what she needs to learn." She looked at Miss Stevens hopefully. "Can you help us?"

Miss Stevens looked thoughtful. "You are a very good friend, Samantha. I think you will be a good teacher, too. Come sit down."

Samantha sat on the chair next to her teacher's desk, and Miss Stevens went to a bookshelf at the side of the room. She came back with four books. "These are the second grade books," she said. "There's a speller, a reader, an arithmetic book, and a geography book." Miss Stevens began writing in the books with a pencil. "I'm marking parts in each of them. Do you think you can help your friend learn them?"

"Yes, Miss Stevens," Samantha said.

"Good," Miss Stevens replied. "Now, stop and see me after school on Friday. Tell me how much your friend has done, and I will help you plan for the following week. It's going to mean quite a bit of work, Samantha. Do you think you can do it?"

"Oh, yes. We can do it!" Samantha stood up, reached for the books, and dashed out of the classroom.

Samantha ran most of the way home. She was so eager to get started that she almost forgot to curtsy when she burst into Grandmary's sitting room. She remembered and bobbed quickly, just in time to avoid her grandmother's frown.

"Grandmary, may I start a school?" asked Samantha in a rush.

Even though Grandmary was used to the unexpected from Samantha, she could still be surprised. She raised an eyebrow and looked at her granddaughter. "Why, Samantha, are you quite sure you've learned all that Miss Stevens has to teach you?"

Samantha tried to explain. "Grandmary, I want to start a school for Nellie. She's having a terrible time at the public school. The teacher is mean to her, and the children tease her because she's just in second grade. But if I helped her, she could move up to the third grade really fast. I just know she could."

Grandmary thought for a minute before she answered. "I'm glad that you are willing to help Nellie," Grandmary said. "But you must not take up too much of her time, Samantha. Nellie has duties at the Van Sicklens' house, and I know you would not want her to neglect them."

"I won't take too much time, I promise," said Samantha. "And we'll be so quiet you won't even know we're here." A little smile crept around Grandmary's mouth, and Samantha knew she had won.

"Very well," said Grandmary. "I guess it won't do any harm."

"Thank you, Grandmary," said Samantha as she hugged her grandmother quickly. Then she hurried out of the room to get her school ready.

It was past four o'clock when Samantha went into the Van Sicklens' back yard looking for Nellie. Samantha couldn't see anyone around, but she could hear someone in the laundry room. She peeked inside and saw Nellie ironing clothes. Nellie worked at a table in the middle of the room. Next to her, three irons sat on a small coal stove. Nellie was sweating with the heat. She put the iron she was using back on the stove and picked up a hot one before she noticed Samantha. Her face brightened when she saw her friend.

"Can you come over to my house?" asked Samantha.

"Oh, not now," Nellie said as she wiped her face with the corner of her apron. "I have to finish the ironing first. But I'm pretty near done." She looked down at her basket. "I can come in about a half-hour."

"All right," Samantha said. "I'll wait for you on my back steps." She walked back to her house and sat with a book until she saw Nellie coming through the hedge.

Nellie was carrying Lydia, the beautiful doll that Samantha had given her. Lydia was no longer quite so fine. Her dress was wrinkled and worn because she had been held so often. Her hair was mussed because Nellie hugged her so tightly at night. Her china hands and face were dirty because Nellie took her with her wherever she could. Samantha looked at Lydia and knew she had been loved. "Come on, Nellie. I have something to show you," she said.

Together, the two girls went inside. In the hallway next to the kitchen, Samantha opened a door that led to a curving stairway. She started up, and Nellie followed. The stairs ended on the second floor, at the back of Grandmary's house. Samantha opened another door. The steps were narrower now. They ended in the attic. Samantha led the way down a narrow hall, past Elsa's room and Jessie's sewing room, to a third stairway. These steps were very steep, and sunlight poured down from above them.

As the girls climbed, Nellie's heart beat faster. She knew where they were now. Samantha was taking her to the small tower that rose above her house and made it look like a palace among the houses of Mount Bedford. Nellie held her breath as she followed Samantha up.

And suddenly they were there—in a tiny room above the world. There was a window in each of the four walls, and Nellie hurried to peer out of each one in turn. She could see all the way down the hill to School Street. She could see the Rylands' house and the Van Sicklens'. And she could see over the trees on the hill. Nellie had never been up so high before. She thought it felt like flying.

When she turned around, Nellie saw that the room was special inside, too. Samantha's small blackboard was there, standing on wooden legs like an easel. There were cushions to sit on, and books stacked neatly against one wall. And there was a small jar of dried white beans.

Nellie was amazed. "Samantha, what . . . ?"

"Here, sit down. We're going to get you out of the second grade, Nellie. Put Lydia on the window seat and let's get started." Samantha opened a book to the place Miss Stevens had marked. "Why don't you start reading there, and when you come to a word you don't know, I'll write it on the blackboard so you can practice it."

Nellie read two pages and Samantha wrote eleven words on the blackboard. Nellie copied them in her copybook to take home and study.

Next they worked on penmanship. Samantha thought this might be difficult for Nellie. She remembered how hard it had been to make her own letters small enough, and how she had worked

*Samantha opened a book to
the place Miss Stevens had marked.*

24

to get all the curls in the right places. But Nellie was fascinated by the letters. She loved the fancy look of them. Even though her first letters were crooked, she kept trying and trying to make them beautiful. Finally it was Samantha who said it was time to stop. They would have to go on to arithmetic.

Samantha spilled some beans out of the jar and onto the floor. She began arranging them in rows. "All right, Nellie, here are seven beans and here are five," she said. "Now, if you add them together—"

"Twelve," Nellie interrupted.

Samantha looked up, startled. She moved more beans into place. "Fourteen and nine," she said.

"Twenty-three," said Nellie, without bothering to count the beans.

Samantha scooped the beans back into the jar and said, "Seventeen and fifteen."

"Thirty-two," Nellie answered promptly.

Samantha sat back on her heels and stared at Nellie. "How did you know that?"

Nellie shrugged. "Lots of times in the city I did the shopping for Mama. I usually had just about a dollar, and I had to get food for all of us. I had to know how many pennies things cost. I had to know how many pennies I had left. And I had to know fast."

Samantha nodded slowly. She didn't want to think about Nellie counting pennies for food. She shoved the bean jar into a corner. "It's getting too late to look at the geography book now. We'll have to save that for another day," she said.

As the girls were stacking the books and getting ready to leave, Samantha had a thought. "You know, Nellie," she said, "we should have a name for our school. I think we should call it the Mount Better School." Her smile had mischief in it as she looked at Nellie. "We've got better students than the Mount Bedford School."

A grin flashed across Nellie's face. "We've got better teachers, too," she said.

THE CONTEST

The next morning, Miss Crampton made an announcement. "The Mount Bedford Ladies Club will be sponsoring the Young People's Speaking Contest again this year. The contest will be held on October fifth in the Mount Bedford Opera House. This year's subject is 'Progress in America,' " she said.

"Students from Lessing's Boys School and from the public elementary school will compete in the contest," Miss Crampton continued. "Our own Academy has been asked to send two girls to take part. In order to choose those two girls, we shall have a contest of our own three weeks from today.

Each of you will prepare and present a speech. Miss Stevens and I shall choose the two best speeches.

"Think very carefully about progress in America," Miss Crampton went on. "Think of all the inventions that have changed our lives—the telephone, the steam engine, electric lights, and so many more. Talk to your parents and read books to get ideas. You have just three weeks to work on your speeches. You should begin today. And remember, I expect excellence."

By the time Miss Crampton finished, all the girls were thinking hard. And by lunchtime everyone was buzzing about the speaking contest.

"If you win," said Helen, "the mayor gives you the medal. Right up on the stage with everybody watching."

"It wouldn't matter if the *President* gave me a medal," said Ida glumly. "I get so nervous in front of people I can hardly remember my name. I could never give a speech in public."

"You get your name in the paper if you win, too," Helen added.

"I would probably just faint and fall off the stage onto the mayor," said Ida. "And my parents would be so embarrassed they'd have to leave town."

"I don't get nervous," said Ruth, "but I don't know enough big words to win. Judges always like big words."

"I'm going to keep smelling salts in my pocket," said Ida. "Remember them if I faint."

"Samantha's going to win," said one of the other girls. "Her essays are always the best, and she won't be scared on the stage."

Samantha shrugged modestly. "I wish I *could* win," she said. She knew she would certainly try. Wouldn't it be wonderful to be up on that stage and feel that medal in her hand?

"Edith Eddleton might win, though." It was Ruth speaking. Ruth was Samantha's friend, but she was an honest friend. "Edith knows more big words than the rest of us put together. And she's not scared of anything."

The other girls groaned. Helen made a face.

"Ruth," she said, "just be quiet and eat your sandwich."

 At three o'clock, Nellie and her sisters waited for Samantha on the front steps of Mount Bedford Public School. This afternoon there were no tears.

"How was it, Nellie?" called Samantha as the three bounded down the steps.

"It wasn't too bad," answered Nellie. Bridget took Samantha's hand, and the girls started home.

"Did they tease you?" Samantha asked.

"They did some," said Nellie, trying to slow Jenny down. "But I didn't mind so much. The teacher mostly left me alone."

"Can you come to Mount Better School today?" asked Samantha.

Nellie looked uncertainly at Samantha. "I have to clean the parlor and sweep the mats," she said. "But if I get the table set right away, I can come for a little while before I have to serve dinner."

Just then Edith Eddleton came riding past on her bicycle. She looked at the girls and stopped. "Samantha Parkington, does your grandmother know you're walking home with *servant* girls?"

30

*"Samantha Parkington, does your grandmother know
you're walking home with servant girls?" Edith asked.*

31

Samantha was shocked. "What are you talking about?"

Edith was only too glad to go on. "Those are Mrs. Van Sicklen's servants. I know *my* mother doesn't want *me* to spend time with them. But then, I guess some people just aren't very particular." And Edith climbed back on her bicycle and pedaled away.

Nellie's face got very red. For once Samantha was speechless. She grabbed Bridget's hand tightly and marched up the sidewalk with long, angry steps. "You know, Nellie," Samantha finally said, "Edith Eddleton is even nastier than Eddie Ryland!"

That evening, Samantha had dinner with Grandmary. Samantha always loved the glitter of the silver and the crystal in the dining room. She loved the little silver bell Grandmary let her ring to tell Mrs. Hawkins to clear the table and bring dessert. She loved the special grown-up time she shared with Grandmary.

Of course such a grown-up dinner wasn't easy. Samantha had to use her very best manners. She sat very straight and kept her napkin in her lap. She tilted her soup spoon away from her in her soup plate. She never spilled or dropped a crumb. She kept her elbows close to her sides, and she tried not to speak until she was spoken to.

Samantha waited until Grandmary asked her about school before she told about the speaking contest. "What do you think is the best sign of progress in America, Grandmary?" Samantha asked.

Grandmary paused for a moment. "First of all, Samantha," she said, "I think it is a mistake to assume that change means progress. The world got along quite well without all these new inventions and machines. Many of them have caused more confusion than they're worth."

Grandmary paused again. "Still," she said, "I think you'd have to say that the telephone has been of some help. Of course it will never take the place of a courteous letter. But I think it does help Mrs. Hawkins when she orders meats and groceries. And it is a comfort if we should ever need the doctor or the fire department. Yes, I think I'd say the telephone is a useful invention."

Samantha had something else she wanted to talk about. But once again she had to wait until Grandmary noticed and asked, "Is something bothering you, Samantha?"

"Grandmary, why isn't Edith Eddleton allowed to play with Nellie?" Samantha asked.

Grandmary looked surprised. "Why, Samantha," she said. "Edith is a young *lady*."

Samantha thought that was ridiculous. But all she said was, "You let me play with Nellie."

"You are *helping* Nellie," said Grandmary, "not playing with her. There is a difference."

Samantha was quiet. She didn't like the difference.

CHAPTER
FIVE
—

PROGRESS

Samantha was delighted that Uncle
Gard came to visit on Saturday. She
was even more pleased to see that he
had not brought his friend Cornelia with him. That
meant that after tea with Grandmary, Samantha
could have him all to herself.

The net was set up for lawn tennis. Samantha
served the ball over the net. Uncle Gard dived for it
and hit it back. Samantha swung her racquet and
missed.

"Uncle Gard," Samantha called as she brought
the ball back and moved closer to the net, "I need
to know about progress. I need to know for the
speaking contest. Two girls from Miss Crampton's

can enter. The winner gets a gold medal. Oh, Uncle Gard, I really want to win. Can you help me?"

Uncle Gard whistled. "That's a pretty big order. What do you need to know?"

"What's the best invention?" Samantha asked.

Her uncle thought a minute. "Well, electric lights are important, Sam. They make a big difference at night. And more and more people are  getting them. I expect someday people will just have electric lights and we won't need gas lamps at all. And what about the automobile? Now that's an important invention. People can go anywhere in automobiles."

"That's silly, Uncle Gard," said Samantha. "You can't go anywhere far away from a drug store or you won't be able to get gasoline."

"Well, that's not a problem," said Uncle Gard. "Just take enough gasoline with you."

"And you can't go anywhere on a rainy day," said Samantha. "Automobiles get stuck in the mud."

"Have a heart, Sam," laughed Uncle Gard. "I thought you *liked* automobiles."

36

"I do," said Samantha as she got ready to hit the ball again. "But they're just not as much fun as horses."

"Why not?"

Samantha reached high and sent the ball sailing. "You can't feed carrots to an automobile!"

For two weeks, Samantha worked hard to learn about progress in America. She read books about new inventions. She took notes about the ideas she got from talking to different people. Mrs. Hawkins said the best invention was the gas stove because it didn't get full of ashes like a coal stove, and you didn't have to keep coals hot all night and all summer. She said that was progress. And Hawkins told Samantha about factories. He said factories were the most important sign of progress in America because there was no end to what they could make. He said they made things fast and they made things cheap. And he said that meant there were more things for more people all over the country. And that started Samantha thinking.

Every afternoon Samantha and Nellie had school in the tower room. Samantha wrote parts of her speech in her copybook and read them aloud to see how they sounded. Then she put the words a different way and read them aloud again. Nellie worked on reading, geography, and spelling. But she knew how much Samantha wanted to win the speaking contest, and she tried not to disturb her.

One afternoon when Nellie was walking home with Samantha, they saw Edith Eddleton standing on the sidewalk with Clarisse Van Sicklen. And Clarisse and Edith saw them. "There's Samantha Parkington keeping company with the servants again," said Edith. She spoke very loudly. "Do you suppose she's practicing to be a washwoman?"

Clarisse answered just as loudly, "Oh, no. I think Nellie is teaching her how to speak for the contest."

"Well of course, that's it," said Edith. "Maybe we should all take lessons." And Edith and Clarisse snickered loudly.

Samantha ignored them and took Nellie's hand. But when they had walked on and could still hear the girls laughing behind them, Samantha said through clenched teeth, "Oh, Nellie, I wish girls were allowed to fight. I most surely do."

Later that afternoon, when Samantha and Nellie were working in Mount Better School, they needed more pencils. Samantha went downstairs to the library to get one from Grandmary's desk. On her way back she heard voices in the parlor. Even without looking at the calling cards on the hall table, Samantha knew who was visiting Grandmary. She recognized Mrs. Eddleton's high shrill voice and Mrs. Ryland's rasping one. And she thought she heard Nellie's name.

Samantha moved closer to the door and peeked through a crack. Mrs. Eddleton was speaking. "Well, the entire neighborhood is simply shocked," she said.

Mrs. Ryland said, "Imagine bringing that whole ragged family to live right here, right in our neighborhood. I just don't know what got into Mrs. Van Sicklen."

"Actually, it was my idea," said Grandmary calmly as she poured the tea. "I urged Mrs. Van Sicklen to give them a home. Their life in the city was quite dreadful." She passed the tea to her guests. "I believe Mrs. Van Sicklen is quite pleased with them. They are all good workers."

The two visitors looked a little embarrassed, but Mrs. Eddleton continued, "My Edith says they are simply filthy, practically in rags."

"They are poor, of course," answered Grandmary. "But I have always found them as clean as any children, and surprisingly well-mannered." Grandmary's back was very straight. Samantha recognized the frosty look in her eye that should have warned the visitors to be careful. But the visitors were too busy talking to notice.

Then Mrs. Ryland asked, "Do you really think it's wise to let Samantha spend so much time with them?"

"I believe Samantha is doing them a great deal of good," said Grandmary. "And it is our duty to do good where we can." She put her teacup down.

Grandmary had the frosty look in her eye
that should have warned the visitors to be careful.

"Would you care for more tea, ladies?" she asked in a voice that was more polite than friendly.

Samantha turned and hurried back up the hall. Suddenly she wanted to be close to Nellie.

After lunch on Thursday, all the girls in Miss Crampton's Academy filed quietly into the assembly room. They stood in front of their chairs until they had sung a hymn and said a prayer. Then they sat down with their backs straight and their hands folded in their laps. There was no whispering even before Miss Crampton began speaking.

"As you know, two girls from this Academy will represent all of us at the Speaking Contest tomorrow evening," Miss Crampton said. "Today, Miss Stevens and I will choose those two girls. They will be the two girls who give the best speeches about progress in America."

Even with her hands folded, Samantha managed to cross her fingers. She took deep breaths to steady herself.

Miss Crampton continued. "I know that everyone in Miss Stevens' class has worked very hard on a speech. And I know we are all very eager to hear the results of this hard work. So I will say nothing more. Helen Whitney, will you please come forward?"

Helen walked up, curtsied, and gave her speech. Then each of the other girls in Samantha's class spoke. Some of their voices were shaky. Ida Dean spoke so softly the audience could barely hear her. But she didn't faint.

At last Samantha's turn came. She was the last girl to speak. Her voice was clear and steady.

"Factories in Modern America," she began. "American factories are the finest in the world. They are true signs of our progress. It used to take many hours to make a pair of shoes or a table by hand. Now machines can make hundreds of shoes and hundreds of tables in just a few hours. And they make thread and cloth, toys and bicycles, furniture, and even automobiles. These things cost less money than they used to because they are made by machines. So now more people can buy the things they want and the things they need. That is progress. Truly, we could not go forward into the twentieth century without our factories and without our machines. They are the greatest sign of progress in America."

There was applause in the room. Miss Stevens nodded in approval. Samantha beamed as she walked back to her seat.

Miss Crampton looked immensely pleased as she stepped to the front of the room. "All of our young ladies have done a splendid job," she said. "I am proud of each one of them. And now, it gives me great pleasure to announce our winners. Will Miss Samantha Parkington please step forward."

Samantha rose and walked to the front of the room again. Miss Crampton handed her an award. The certificate was crisp and smooth in her hand. She felt her heart swell with pleasure as she heard the applause around her.

When the clapping stopped, Miss Crampton announced the other winner. It was Edith Eddleton.

CHAPTER SIX

WINNERS

In Mount Better School that afternoon, Nellie watched proudly as Samantha pinned her award to the wall. "Can I hear your speech, Samantha?" Nellie asked. There was no doubt in Nellie's mind that her friend's speech would be the best ever written since Abraham Lincoln's.

Samantha cleared her throat and used her most proper voice. She repeated her speech just as she had at the Academy, remembering with a thrill the applause that had followed it. She finished proudly and then looked at Nellie for the praise she was sure would be coming.

But Nellie was staring at the floor and running

45

her finger along the edge of the cushion.

"Well?" asked Samantha.

"It's very nice," said Nellie in a voice that said it really wasn't nice at all.

Samantha felt hurt. "What's the matter with it?" she asked.

"It's very nice. It's just . . . well, it's just not very true," said Nellie.

"What do you mean?"

"I used to work in a factory, Samantha. It's not like that."

Nellie *had* worked in a factory. Samantha had almost forgotten that. "Well, what's a factory like, then?" she asked.

Nellie was quiet. She was remembering things she didn't want to remember. "I worked in a big room with other kids," she said finally. "Twenty others, I guess. But that didn't make it fun. We couldn't play. We couldn't even talk. The machines were too noisy. They were so noisy that when I got home at night my ears were buzzing and it was a long time before I could hear anything. We had to go to work at seven in the morning, and we worked until seven at night. Every day but Sunday."

Nellie continued, "I worked on the machines that
wound the thread. There were hundreds of spools.
We had to put in new ones when the old ones got
full, and we tied the thread if it broke. We had to
stand up all the time. I got so tired, Samantha.
My back hurt and my legs hurt and my arms
got heavy. The machines got fuzz and dust all over
everything. It was in the air, and it got in my
mouth and made it hard to breathe."

Nellie was quiet again. Then she went on. "The
room was awful hot in summer. But it was worse in
winter because there wasn't any heat. Our feet

nearly froze. We couldn't wear shoes."

Samantha was shocked. "You couldn't wear shoes?" she asked.

"We had to climb on the machines to change the spools, and shoes could make us slip. The machines were so strong they could break your hand or your foot or pull a finger off as easy as anything. We all had to have our hair short. If your hair was long the machines could catch it and pull it right out. They just kept winding. Once I saw that happen to a girl. She was just standing there, and then suddenly she was screaming and half her head was bleeding. She almost died."

Nellie was running her finger along the edge of the cushion again. "They paid us one dollar and eighty cents a week." She looked straight at her friend. "That's why thread is so cheap."

Samantha stared at Nellie. She couldn't move. She felt numb and cold. Only her scalp was tingling and her arms had a strange ache in them.

48

The Mount Bedford Opera House was used for most of the town's special events. It served Mount Bedford for everything from roller skating parties to concerts. On the evening of the Young People's Speaking Contest it was filled with wooden chairs.

The contest speakers sat on the stage, facing parents and friends from all over town. Grandmary sat in the second row, wearing a gray silk dress and looking calm and stately. Nellie sat with her mother near the back of the room. She looked shy and out of place.

As the president of the Mount Bedford Ladies Club stepped to the front of the stage, smiling and bobbing her head, the room grew quiet. She welcomed everyone, then introduced the speakers and told what schools they represented. Then it was time for the speeches.

One of the boys from Lessing's School told about a new building that was twenty stories high. He said that from now on all cities would be different because of it. Another boy talked about automobiles, and someone spoke about electric lights. A girl from the public school talked about medicine. She said people didn't get sick as much as they used to. Then it was Edith Eddleton's turn.

Edith walked to the front of the stage like an army general. She paused for a moment with her head a little to one side. Then she boomed out her speech in a voice meant to reach the Opera House doors and beyond.

"We are indeed fortunate to live in this age of progress. Progress is the great American adventure. In the old days, a man had to work all day and all night to support himself and his family. But now, in modern America, great machines can be a great benefit to everyone. Now everyone can have all he needs without a difficult struggle. Fortunes can be made now as never before. Now, with the help of machines, anyone can become wealthy. What a great opportunity man has in the twentieth century. Are we not fortunate to live in this great age of progress?"

Everyone clapped loudly as Edith returned to her chair in triumph. She sat down, smoothed her dress, and smiled at Samantha.

Then Samantha heard her name called. She walked to the front of the stage calmly. She didn't look at Miss Crampton and Miss Stevens. She knew what they were expecting her to say. But she had learned something more about factories from Nellie, and now she had something else to say. Samantha stood tall and looked straight ahead. In her mind she could hear the words she had been practicing ever since her last lesson in Mount Better School.

"Americans are very proud of being modern," Samantha began. "We are proud of our progress. We are proud of the machines in our factories because they make so many new things for us. But Americans are proud of being truthful, too. If we were truthful we would say that the factory machines make things fast and cheap, but they are dangerous, too. They can hurt the children who work in the factories. The machines can break their arms. They can cut off their fingers. They can make children sick. And children who work in factories don't have time to play or go to school. They are too tired." Samantha spoke calmly and clearly. She had discovered something. She had discovered that it is easy to talk to people, even to many people, if you really believe what you are saying.

"If our factories can hurt children, then we have not made good progress in America,"

Samantha had discovered that it is easy to talk to people,
even to many people, if you really believe what you are saying.

Samantha continued. "And I believe Americans want to be good. I believe we want to be kind. And if we are kind, I believe we will take care of the children. Then we can truly be proud of our factories and our progress."

As Samantha walked back to her chair at the end of her speech, there was a long silence. Grandmary looked a little shocked. How could Samantha have known about such things? Then Grandmary looked back at Nellie. Nellie was sitting with her back straight and her eyes shining. And Grandmary understood. She understood a great deal. A proud smile spread across her face and she began to applaud. Her applause joined the clapping that began all over the room and grew into a long, loud roar of approval.

Edith Eddleton looked rather like a snowman that had been left too long in the sun.

The next time Samantha and Nellie sat in Mount Better School, it was not for a lesson. It was for a celebration. Samantha's first-prize medal hung from its blue ribbon on the schoolroom wall.

The girls were eating cookies and little cakes with pink frosting. Mrs. Hawkins had made them a whole pitcher of lemonade. They sat on cushions, with napkins spread on their laps, feeling very pleased with themselves.

Nellie sighed happily as she finished a cookie. She leaned back against the wall. "I'm glad we're celebrating today, Samantha. Something nice happened to me, too."

"Oh?" said Samantha, eager to share her friend's good news. "What?"

Nellie smiled shyly. "I moved to third grade."

Samantha jumped up, spun around, and clapped her hands. "Nellie, that's wonderful! That's just wonderful!" Then she stopped and looked at her friend. Nellie didn't look as happy as she should. "You didn't tell me right away, Nellie. What's wrong?" asked Samantha.

Nellie looked down at her napkin. Then she looked back at Samantha. "I have the desk next to Eddie Ryland."

Samantha's eyes grew wide and she sank back to the floor. "Ooohh, Nellie," she said with feeling.

Both girls were quiet for a minute. Then Samantha pushed the cookies away and reached for a book. "Hurry up and finish your lemonade. We've got to start studying. You've got to move up to the head of the class!"

Private academy

From the outside, you might not guess that Samantha's school was a school at all. Miss Crampton's Academy for Young Ladies looked like a house because that's what it was—a house with two or three rooms set aside as classrooms. In 1904 many girls from wealthy families like Samantha's studied in private *academies* that met in the headmistress' house. These schools were usually small. There wasn't room for more than ten or twelve desks in a classroom the size of your bedroom! Often there were just three or four girls in each grade, and several grades shared one classroom and one teacher.

In most private academies, students were either all girls or all boys. Girls in private academies studied reading, spelling, history, arithmetic, and geography. *Penmanship,* or handwriting, was an important subject, too. Students practiced holding their pens properly and making fancy letters like these. They were not allowed to turn in messy written work with drips of ink on it. That could be difficult, because their pens often leaked.

Some private academies made lunch a lesson, too. They served a fancy meal in the dining room and students practiced good table manners. After lunch, many academy students practiced dancing, French, drawing,

Art class, 1904

and even how to walk, talk, sit, and bend gracefully. These were considered important lessons for young ladies.

Public school, 1904

But in 1904 not every girl in the United States was a young lady who went to a private academy. Private schools were expensive. Many more American girls went to the free public schools in their neighborhoods, where they studied most of the same subjects that Samantha did. In public schools boys and girls went to school together. There were usually 20 or 30 children in each class. Students in the same grade were about the same age. But in the poor neighborhoods of large cities some children did not go to school at all because they had to work. Even though there were laws that said children should not work, some poor children

Students from a city school

diseobeyed them so they could earn
money to help their families. Some
children tried to work during the
day and go to school at night, but
many times they were too tired and
fell asleep at their desks.

Child worker in factory

No matter where they went to
school, students were expected to be quiet and obedi-
ent in the classroom. In an academy like Miss Crampton's, students who misbehaved might be sent home
with a note from the teacher. In a public school, the
punishment was usually harsher. Teachers swatted
students with paddles or rulers, made them kneel in a
corner, and slapped or boxed their ears. Many
teachers believed that these punishments taught

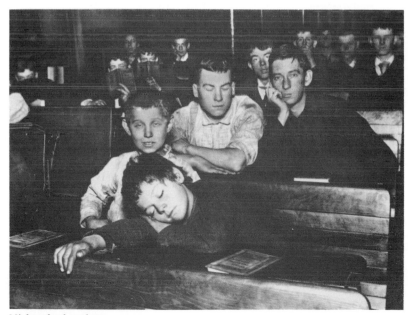

Night school students

lessons that were just as important as arithmetic, geography, and history.

Reading books were supposed to teach more than reading, too. They showed how polite, honest girls and boys always ended up better off than rude, dishonest

children. And students like Samantha and Nellie were often asked to write essays or speeches about right and wrong. Sometimes they memorized their speeches and recited them in front of the whole class or the whole school.

Going to school in 1904 often meant sitting quietly, memorizing, and reciting. But some teachers believed children learned more by doing things. These teachers taught science by doing experiments. For instance, students in their classes took flowers apart to learn about plants.

Exercise was also an important part of the school day. Between classes students did yawning and stretching exercises at their desks because teachers thought this made them healthier. During noon recess

Swimming lessons without water!

they played games like baseball. They had lessons in archery and tennis, played basketball, and even learned how to swim.

In 1904 American children were supposed to go to school until they were 16 years old. However, most of the boys and girls who started school never finished eighth grade. Most children went to school for as long as they could, then began working in factories and stores, on farms and in mines. Some students did go on to high school, and a few went to college. But a college education was still an unusual privilege, even for a wealthy girl like Samantha.

College graduates

61

THE AMERICAN GIRLS COLLECTION®

There are more books in The American Girls Collection. They're filled with the adventures that four lively American girls—Felicity, Kirsten, Samantha, and Molly—lived long ago.

But the books are only part of The American Girls Collection—only the beginning. There are lovable dolls—Felicity, Kirsten, Samantha, and Molly dolls—that have beautiful clothes and lots of wonderful accessories. They make these stories of the past come alive today for American girls like you.

To learn about The American Girls Collection, fill out this postcard and mail it to Pleasant Company. We will send you a catalogue about all the books, dolls, dresses, and other delights in The American Girls Collection.

I'm an American girl who loves to get mail.
Please send me a catalogue of The American Girls Collection®:

My name is _____

My address is _____

City _____ State _____ Zip _____

My Birthday is _____ My age is ____

I am in ____ grade.   Parent's Signature _____

The book this postcard is in came from:

☐ a school book club   ☐ a school book fair

☐ a school library   ☐ a friend or relative

If the postcard has already
been removed from this book
and you would like to receive
a Pleasant Company catalogue,
please send your name and
address to:

PLEASANT COMPANY
P.O. Box 995
MIDDLETON, WI 53562-9979
or call our toll-free number
1-800-845-0005